D0538729

Disney's

GOOF TROOP

Great Egg-Spectations

Adapted by Janet Gilbert
Illustrated by Don Williams
Painted by Jim Story and H. R. Russell

A GOLDEN BOOK • NEW YORK
Western Publishing Company, Inc., Racine, Wisconsin 53404

Library of Congress Catalog Card Number: 92-70286 ISBN: 0-307-00123-7   MCMXCIII

"It's not fair!" Max grumbled. He was standing on the shore of Fossil Lake, where he had just freed the wild duck that had been his pet. His father said he had to let the duck go. Poor Max! His father never liked the pets he brought home.

Just then Max noticed something large and pink
and purple.

"It's a giant egg! But where's the mama?" he said
to himself.

Max looked around for a large bird, one that could be
the egg's mother. There wasn't a bird in sight, so he decided
to take the egg home. "It needs me!" Max declared, happily
lifting the big egg.

When Max got home, his dad was busy cooking supper. "That you, son?" Goofy called.

"Uh, hi, Dad," Max said quickly as he hurried through the kitchen. He struggled up to his room with the egg.

"I won't tell Dad about the egg yet," thought Max. "But wait until I show PJ!"

Max called his best friend and told him to come over right away. PJ lived next door.

PJ was shocked when he saw the egg.

"If that thing hatches, the bird is going to be huge!" he exclaimed. "Will your dad let you keep it?"

"I hope so," Max replied with a sigh. To keep the egg warm, Max covered it with a blanket and earmuffs. Then he and PJ went downstairs to eat. PJ was staying for supper.

While Max and PJ were eating, strange things started to happen to the egg. First it began to shake.

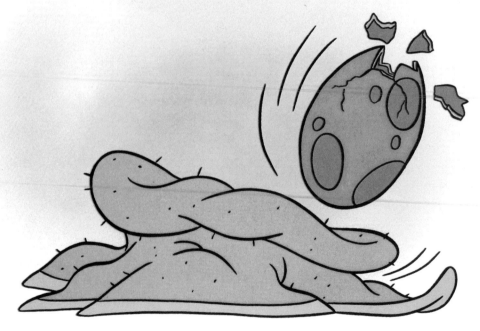

Then it began to crack.

Finally a scaly green head poked out. *"Gronk!"* the creature cried. Bit by bit, it began to break out of the shell.

When Max and PJ went back upstairs, they couldn't
believe their eyes.

"It looks like a b-baby d-dinosaur!" PJ sputtered.

Max was so happy. He had a new pet.

"Gronk!" the dinosaur gurgled.

PJ gulped. "I'm outta here," he said, dashing for the door. "Good luck, Maxie!"

Max patted the baby dinosaur. "I bet you would like a bath," he said gently. "Let's sneak you into the bathroom before Dad comes up."

"Gee, I wonder what I should name you?" said Max as his new pet splashed in the tub. "I bet you're a boy dinosaur."

Just then the baby dinosaur dunked his head in the water and started blowing bubbles.

"I've got it! I'll call you Bubbles," said Max. "Now if only I could figure out a way to tell Dad about you . . ."

Late that night Bubbles left Max sleeping in his room to go exploring. Soon he poked his green head into Goofy's room. Goofy was snoring so loudly that the windows were rattling.

Bubbles crept closer to the bed to see what was making all the noise.

To Bubbles, Goofy looked just like Max! When he saw
Goofy, he gave him a big, friendly lick. Goofy slowly opened
his sleepy eyes.

"A monster!" Goofy screamed, seeing Bubbles. He leapt out of bed in terror.

As he jumped, a lamp fell to the floor with a crash.

"Arp! Arp!" Bubbles whimpered, scared by the noisy commotion.

The noise woke Max up. He rushed to Goofy's room to see what was going on.

"Stay back, son!" Goofy warned.

"Don't hurt him, Dad!" Max cried. "He's my pet!"

"Your *what*?" yelled Goofy. Max quickly told his father the whole story about Bubbles. Then he begged to keep him.

"But he's some kind of dinosaur, son," said Goofy. "He belongs in a museum, or in a zoo!"

"I'll take good care of him," Max pleaded. "I promise!"

Finally Goofy gave in. "Aw, shucks, you can keep him as long as he stays out of trouble," he said, "and doesn't get too big!"

Max beamed. "No problem," he said happily. "I mean, how big can he get?"

In no time at all, Bubbles grew *very* big. He loved food, especially marshmallows. Finally Goofy had had enough.

"He's eaten a thousand bags of marshmallows, four hundred cabbages, ten houseplants, and the remote control," Goofy said with a groan. "Sorry, son, but we just can't keep him anymore. And it's not fair to keep Bubbles cooped up in the house like this anyway."

Max knew his dad was right. "Okay," he said sadly. "I'll take him back to Fossil Lake tomorrow."

Late that night, while Max and Goofy were sleeping, Bubbles woke up and wandered outside. He was hungry. He found a tasty shrub in PJ's front yard.

Munch, munch, munch! Bubbles chewed so loudly that Pete woke up. Pete was PJ's dad.

"Who's out there?" Pete shouted from the bedroom window.

Max and Goofy heard the noise, too. They ran outside and saw Pete chasing Bubbles with a broom. PJ was up and chasing his father.

Max was scared. "Dad, we gotta save Bubbles!" he cried.

Goofy had an idea. He and Max jumped into their old jalopy and took off. Goofy headed straight for Fossil Lake.

"But, Dad!" Max shouted. "They went the other way!"

"Don't worry," said Goofy, and he zoomed on down the road.

Meanwhile Bubbles ran until he was trapped in a
dead end alley.

"Gotcha!" Pete growled. "You miserable monster."

"Don't hurt him," PJ begged. "He's just a baby!"

Suddenly they heard a terrifying roar behind them.

It was a dinosaur as big as a house, with Goofy and Max
on top.

"Bubbles, meet your mama," said Max with a grin.

The giant dinosaur lowered her head and nuzzled
Bubbles on the cheek.

"Where did you find her?" asked PJ.

"I figured if there was an egg at the lake, there had to be a mama somewhere," Goofy said proudly.

Pete looked dazed. Two dinosaurs in one night were too much for him.

"I'd better get Dad home," said PJ as he led Pete away.

Later Max and Goofy watched as the two dinosaurs swam off into the lake together.

"Max, you took good care of Bubbles," said Goofy. "I'm proud of you. It's time we got you a real pet."

"Great!" said Max. "How about a boa constrictor? Maybe a tarantula?"

"A tarantula!" Goofy choked. "Now, just a gawrsh-darned minute, son . . ."